Supermarket Zoo

For Tinka and Puppy xxx – C.H.
For Becs x – E.E.

SIMON AND SCHUSTER
First published in Great Britain in 2010 by Simon and Schuster UK Ltd
1st Floor, 222 Gray's Inn Road, London WC1X 8HB
A CBS Company

Text copyright © 2010 Caryl Isaac
Illustrations copyright © 2010 Edward Eaves

The right of Caryl Isaac and Edward Eaves to be identified as the author and illustrator of this work has been asserted by them in accordance with the Copyright, Designs and Patents Act, 1988

A CIP catalogue record for this book is available from the British Library upon request

ISBN: 978-1-84738-477-5 (HB)
ISBN: 978-1-84738-478-2 (PB)

Printed in China
10 9 8 7 6 5 4 3 2 1

Supermarket Zoo

Caryl Hart & Ed Eaves

SIMON AND SCHUSTER
London   New York   Sydney

The minute I wake up, I know something is different, but I can't quite figure out what.

It's probably nothing.

So I pick up my ball
and I am just going
out to play when . . .

"Albie!"

It's Mum. She has her car keys in one hand and a pile of bags in the other. This can only mean one thing – **shopping!**

DISASTER!

I HATE shopping!

But Mum has me trapped and there's nothing I can do.

At the supermarket, the first thing
I notice is our trolley. It's **enormous** –
I can't even reach the handle.
And there's a really **funny** smell.

Mum doesn't seem to notice, she just hands me the shopping list and sets off.

6 monkeys

2 giraffes

Fresh lizards

3 kilos tortoises

27 parrots (give or take)

Pride of lions

2 bales of hay

5 tins of lion food

Vegetables, fruit, nuts

Tyr

"Right," says Mum. "Reptiles first.
Chameleons or iguanas? We'll need two."

This is **mad!**
But Mum seems to think it's completely normal.

I pick out two green-and-orange chameleons and place them in the trolley. Mum says, "Gently now, don't bruise them!"

We hurry past the rattlesnakes and cobras, to the tortoises. I spot a sign saying:

**FREE SALAD
WITH EVERY TORTOISE.**

So we take three.

Next we pass the cool cabinets. I say, "Can we get a penguin?" Mum sighs, "OK, but get one from the back because it'll be fresher."

Then this polar bear smiles at me. **"Pleeeease,"** I say. But Mum is cross. "No, not today."

At the giraffes, we pick a
Mother-and-Baby Special.

Then we head off to find some parrots.

I've never heard such **screeching** and **squawking**.
I like the toucans best but Mum says, "It's parrots
or nothing."

People say it's good luck if a bird poops
on your head, but I don't think Mum agrees!

Next on the list are the monkeys.
Now everyone knows monkeys are tricky,
but have you ever tried getting six of them
to sit in a trolley full of pecking parrots?
It's **impossible!**

In the end, I have to open a packet of nuts to keep them all quiet.

Then we get to the lions.
Now, I love watching big cats on TV, but to look straight into
the wide eyes of a hungry lion, **well that's something else!**

Mum chooses one of the meanest looking beasts I've ever seen. "I'll go and find the lion food," I say. Not that I'm scared or anything.

We pile in bags of carrots, monkey nuts, bananas, seeds and mangoes. By the time we get to the check-out the trolley is so **heavy** I can hardly push it.

Mum heaves our shopping onto the conveyor belt while I start to pack.

It's a **big** job.

We are nearly done when Mum rushes off shouting, "Keep going, I won't be a minute!" She always forgets **something** . . .

But I wasn't expecting this!

Outside, we open the car. It looks so small.
It's lucky that mums are so good at packing
or we'd have never got everything in.

Well, I told you this morning that I thought something was different – and it turns out I was right! This has been the best shopping trip ever. Just look at all my new friends! **I wonder what we'll buy next week . . .**

Things to buy from
the Monster Market:

2 spotted furzelwurzels

3 bouncing bongle tweezles

3 kilos of bug-eyed flomstrops

Warp garglers

Blimps

Noozles or bog-tromplers